15

Christmas

DEC

JA

HOLLY KELLER

Merry Christmas, Geraldine

Greenwillow Books, New York

Geraldine wanted to get a big Christmas tree. "All the way up to the ceiling," she said happily. "That's silly, Geraldine," said Mama, who was busy making cookies.

"Why?" Geraldine asked.

"Because it will be hard for you and Willie to carry a big tree, and a small one is just as pretty."

"But small isn't pretty," Geraldine argued. "And we can carry a big tree."

"Yes, small is very pretty," said Mama, and she kissed the top of Geraldine's head. "But if you don't hurry, you won't get any tree at all."

Geraldine grabbed Willie's hand and pulled
him out the door.

"Let's sing," she said.

"I can't," Willie answered. "I don't know any songs."

"I'll teach you one," said Geraldine. "Just sing what
 I sing:

>*"Jingle Bear, Jingle Bear,*
>*I see Santa's underwear. . . ."*

Willie giggled.

Uncle Albert had a tree stand a few blocks
away.
He waved when he saw Willie and Geraldine
coming down the street.
"Mama sent us to get our Christmas tree,"
Willie explained.
"And what sort of tree are we looking for?"
Uncle Albert asked.
"A big one," Geraldine said, and she made
a face at Willie so that he wouldn't say anything.

Uncle Albert pulled out a tree. "How is this one?"
he asked.

"Good," Willie said.

"Not big enough," Geraldine corrected.

Willie pulled on Geraldine's sleeve, but Geraldine
pretended not to feel it.

Uncle Albert took out another tree, and Geraldine
shook her head.

"That one," she said,
and she pointed to the
biggest tree on the rack.
Uncle Albert laughed.
"How will you
get it home?"
"We can carry it,"
Geraldine said
cheerily. "Isn't
it pretty, Willie?"
"Too big,
Geraldine,"
Willie
whispered.
"It's not,"
Geraldine
whispered
back.

Geraldine took one end and Willie took
the other, but the tree wouldn't budge.

"I'll have to make it just a little shorter,
Geraldine," said Uncle Albert.
"Not too much," Geraldine said.

"It's still too heavy, Geraldine,"
Willie complained after they
had walked a little way.
"Try harder!" Geraldine called back.

"I can't see anything," Willie yelled as they
went past Thistle's vegetable store.
Mr. Thistle laughed. "That's because you
have branches over your eyes!" he said,
and he went to get Mrs. Thistle's big scissors.

"Don't trim too much!" Geraldine pleaded.

When they came to the corner, Geraldine
started to turn.
"Oops!" she cried when she remembered
Willie. Willie let go, but it was too late, and
he skidded into the garbage can.
Willie was so mad that Geraldine had to
give him two "all better" kisses.

Mr. Peters was watching from the window
of his hardware store. He came out carrying
a big saw.
"Now you'll be able to see each other," he said,
and he chuckled.
Geraldine looked away.

A few minutes later Mrs. Wilson came down the
street carrying a basket of Christmas cards that
she was taking to the post office.
"Hello, Geraldine," she said.
Geraldine stopped to let Mrs. Wilson pass.
Willie didn't notice Mrs. Wilson, so he just kept
on walking and ended up on the sidewalk again.

Geraldine helped him brush himself off.
"Come on, Willie," she said. "We're almost home."

Papa was waiting for them at the house. Willie was furious. He dropped his end of the tree and went to find Mama.

"Hmmmm," Papa said when he tried to get the tree
into the house. "This might need a little clipping."
"No," Geraldine said firmly.

Mama came to the door. "Be reasonable,
Geraldine. It's too big."
"It's not," Geraldine insisted.
"But it won't fit," Papa said calmly.
"It will," Geraldine said.

She looked at the tree and at the door.
Then she marched over to the tree, closed
her eyes, counted one-two-three, and
pushed as hard as she could.

"Ohhh," she cried when the tree crashed through the door.

Papa stood the tree up in the living room.
"Perfect," Geraldine announced.
And everybody laughed.

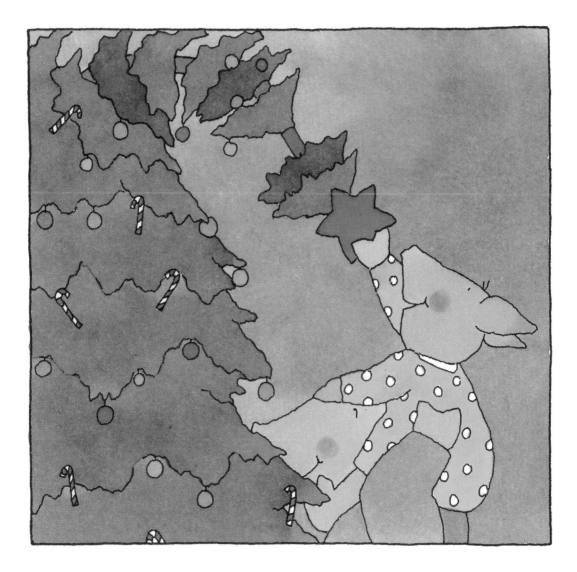

After dinner they decorated the tree with
colored balls and candy canes.
Geraldine had to sit on Papa's shoulders
to put the star on top.
"Merry Christmas," she shouted triumphantly.

"Merry Christmas, Geraldine," Mama and Papa
whispered, because Willie was fast asleep.

JUV
EASY
Keller   Keller, Holly

         Merry Christmas,
         Geraldine

DUE DATE
